This book belongs to:

....

....

....

Retold by Gaby Goldsack
Illustrated by Ruth Galloway (Advocate)
Designed by Jester Designs

Language consultant: Betty Root

ISBN 0-75259-430-3

This is a P³ book
This edition published in 2002

P³
Queen Street House
4 Queen Street
Bath BA1 1HE, UK
Copyright © Exclusive Editions 2002

Printed in China.

p^3

The Gingerbread Man

Helping Your Child Read

Learning to read is an exciting challenge for most children. From a very early age, sharing storybooks with children, talking about the pictures, and guessing what might happen next are all very important parts of the reading experience.

Sharing Reading

Set aside a regular quiet time to share reading with younger children, or to be available to encourage older children as they develop into independent readers.

First Readers are intended to encourage and support the early stages of learning to read. They present well-loved tales that children will enjoy hearing again and again. Familiarity helps children identify some of the words and phrases.

When you feel your child is ready to move ahead, encourage him or her to join in so that you read the story aloud together. Always pause to talk about the pictures. The easy-to-read speech bubbles in **First Readers** provide an excellent "joining-in" activity. The bright, clear illustrations and matching text will help children understand the story.

Building Confidence

In time, children will want to read *to* you. When this happens, be patient and give continual praise. They may not read all the words correctly, but children's substitutions are often very good guesses.

The repetition in each book is especially helpful for building confidence. If your child cannot read a particular word, go back to the beginning of the sentence and read it together so the meaning is not lost. Most importantly, do not continue if your child is tired or just needs a change.

Reading Alone

The next step is for your child to read alone. Try to be available to give help and support. Remember to give lots of encouragement and praise.

Along with other simple stories, **First Readers** will help ensure reading is an enjoyable and rewarding experience for children.

Once upon a time there was a little old man and a little old woman.

One day the little old woman made a gingerbread man.

The little old woman put the gingerbread man in the oven to bake. The little old woman and the little old man waited.

Then the little old man opened the oven. Out jumped the gingerbread man.

He ran off, singing
"Run, run, as fast as you can,
You can't catch me,
I'm the gingerbread man."

The gingerbread man ran on until he
met a cow.

"Stop!" said the cow. "I want to
eat you."

"I have run away from a little old man and a little old woman," laughed the gingerbread man. "And I can run away from you.

"Run, run, as fast as you can,
You can't catch me,
I'm the gingerbread man."

You can't catch me!

The gingerbread man ran on until he met a horse.

"Stop!" said the horse. "I want to eat you."

"I have run away from a little old man, a little old woman, and a cow," laughed the gingerbread man. "And I can run away from you.

"Run, run, as fast as you can,
You can't catch me,
I'm the gingerbread man."

Neigh!

I'm the gingerbread man!

The gingerbread man ran on until he met a farmer.

"Stop!" said the farmer. "I want to eat you."

"I have run away from a little old man, a little old woman, a cow, and a horse," laughed the gingerbread man. "And I can run away from you."

Come back!

He ran so fast that the farmer could not catch him.

"Run, run, as fast as you can,

You can't catch me,

I'm the gingerbread man."

The gingerbread man ran on and on.

He was very proud of his running.

"No one can catch me," he said.

I can run fast!

Then he met a sly old fox. "Come here!" said the fox. "I want to talk to you."

"I have run away from a little old man,
a little old woman, a cow, a horse, and
a farmer," laughed the gingerbread
man. "And I can run away from you.

"Run, run, as fast as you can,

You can't catch me,

I'm the gingerbread man."

I can run away from you!

The fox ran after the gingerbread man.
The gingerbread man ran even faster.

Soon they came to a river. "How will
I cross the river?" asked the
gingerbread man.

"Jump on my tail. I will take you across," said the sly old fox.

The gingerbread man jumped onto the fox's tail.

The fox began to
swim across the river.

Splash!

Soon he said to the gingerbread man,
"My tail is tired. Jump onto my back."

So the gingerbread man did.

Jump on my back!

Jump on my nose!

Then the fox said, "My back is tired.
Jump onto my nose."

So the gingerbread man did.

Soon they reached the other side. The
fox threw the gingerbread man into
the air.

Snap!

Then, gulp, he ate the gingerbread man
in a single bite.

The gingerbread man never ran away again.

Read and Say

How many of these words can you say? The pictures will help you. Look back in your book and see if you can find the words in the story.

cow

farmer

fox

gingerbread man

horse

man

oven

river

woman